Lee Sachse

AVALANCHE!

AVALANCHE!

by
STEPHANIE BAUDET
Illustrated by Kate Rogers

HAMISH HAMILTON
LONDON

First published in Great Britain 1986 by
Hamish Hamilton Children's Books
Garden House 57–59 Long Acre London WC2E 9JZ
Copyright © 1986 by Stephanie Baudet
Illustrations copyright © 1986 by Hamish Hamilton Ltd

British Library Cataloguing in Publication Data
Baudet, Stephanie
 Avalanche! — (Antelope)
 I. Title
 823'.914   PZ7
ISBN 0-241-11734-8

Filmset in Baskerville by
Katerprint Co. Ltd, Oxford
Printed in Great Britain at the
University Press, Cambridge

Chapter 1

"I THINK I saw a cable car!" Jonathan exclaimed, his eyes wide with excitement. "We must be nearly there." He wiped the steamy window with his arm and peered through again, snub nose pressed against the glass.

"About time," said Andrew who was sitting beside him. "We've been four hours on this coach." Despite his complaining he leaned across his friend to get a clearer view.

The girl in front of them flung herself round to kneel on her seat with a thud.

"Never seen a cable car before," she sneered. "I've been on thousands."

Andrew raised his eyebrows and gave her one of his penetrating glares, but Jonathan just stared through the window again. He'd been looking forward to this school ski-ing trip but was already fed up with Melanie Jackson and her boasting. Forty children on the coach and she had to be sitting near him.

"Sit down, Melanie. It's dangerous to kneel up like that."

Jonathan and Andrew exchanged amused glances as their teacher, Mrs Thomas, shouted from two seats back.

Melanie sat down but turned round again, a show-off smile on her face.

"I bet *you'll* be too scared to go in the cable car!" she hissed. "I'm not afraid. I've been ski-ing since I was a baby."

"You still are," said Jonathan under his breath.

She either didn't hear or ignored him as she went on: "My Mum and Dad brought me when I was four months old."

"And I suppose you were the wonder baby of the slopes," said Andrew, sarcastically. "Ski-ing before you could walk."

"'Course not," Melanie gave a genuine giggle. "But anyway," she said, "my Dad says I'm a good skier now and I'm going on all the difficult slopes, the black runs."

"Melanie, will you *please* turn round," came Mrs Thomas' sharp voice again.

Melanie flicked her long brown hair behind her as she turned to face the front again.

At last the coach pulled up in front of the Hotel Suisse and there was a mad scramble to collect belongings and get out into the snow.

Jonathan was relieved to see, as he humped his suitcase into his room, that Melanie's room was on the next floor.

"I bags this bed," said Andrew, throwing his flight bag onto the neatly puffed-up duvet.

"Okay." Jonathan wished he'd been in the room first to claim the bed by the window but he settled for the other one. What did it matter anyhow? It was the ski-ing that mattered. Jonathan had been ski-ing once before, when his mum and dad were still together. It had been a great holiday. He never thought he'd have the chance to ski again but now, here he was, on his first school ski-ing trip.

"Cor, look!" Andrew had flung back the curtain and was looking out of the window at the crisp, white slopes.

"Look Jon. We've got a balcony and we're right beside the chairlift. All we've got to do in the morning is put on our skis and whizz down to there."

They could both just see the chairlift station to their left and the chairs hanging still and empty on their cable, one behind the other, past their window and on up the mountain. Jonathan's eyes followed the jagged ridge of peaks across the horizon, pink-tipped in the sunset. He shivered, with excitement or apprehension he wasn't sure. Tomorrow he would be up there.

"I'm famished. Come on, Jon. Mr Fredericks said dinner was at seven o'clock." Andrew was at the door and turning the handle. "Come *on*."

They went downstairs to the dining room. Just inside the entrance a chef was arranging a huge steaming pie onto a big table spilling over with food.

"Do you just help yourself to as much as you like?" asked Andrew.

"Yes, but go easy now, Barrett. If you eat too much you'll come down those slopes like a giant snowball."

The boys looked round to see the headmaster, Mr Fredericks, smiling good-naturedly. Andrew grinned, not minding the reference to his love of food and his chubbiness.

"It might help me win in the races on Friday, Sir, being the heaviest."

Jonathan heard the teacher laugh above the growing babble of voices as more children swarmed around the table. He filled his own plate with a huge wedge of meat pie, chips and salad and made his way to a vacant table.

Andrew and two others joined him and they all ate in silence, hungry after the long journey.

It was when they were halfway through their second helping of ice-cream that Melanie Jackson paused by their table on her way out of the dining room.

"So, Andrew Barrett, you think you're going to win one of the races, do you?"

"Yeah, I might."

"Huh, they're always on the easy nursery slopes anyway. I bet you and Jonathan will be too scared to do a black run," she taunted.

"I'm not scared," Andrew retorted.

"Nor me," said Jonathan, though his voice sounded somehow as if it didn't belong to him. He felt a twinge of panic inside. He'd had the same feeling when his father had left, and people had said, "You must be the man of the house now . . . look after your mother . . . " How could he do that? He was only ten.

"I bet you don't," Melanie Jackson was saying. And she walked away, whispering and giggling with her friend.

After dinner there were games and quizzes in the lounge and the teachers turned out to be amazingly different people away from school. It was quite late when Andrew and Jonathan got to their room.

Andrew washed in three seconds flat and flung himself onto the bed, exhausted.

Jonathan felt tired too. "Did you bring an alarm clock, Andrew?" he called from the bathroom.

There was no reply and he stepped back to look through the open door. His friend's dark tousled head lay quite still on the pillow, eyes closed, mouth slightly open.

Jonathan grinned. He picked up the wet flannel from the basin, took aim, and threw.

Splat! Andrew jerked up to a sitting position with a yell and looked dazed for a moment as the flannel slipped off his face and on to his pyjamas. Then his eyes focussed on Jonathan and in one movement the flannel came flying back, closely followed by a pillow.

The flannel hit target again but the pillow sailed in through the bathroom door and landed in the bath. Jonathan was by this time beside his own bed, grabbing his pillow, but before he could throw it Andrew was on him and they squealed and laughed as they wrestled each other.

Suddenly the door was flung open.

"Andrew! Jonathan! It's eleven o'clock. Get to bed at once and not another sound!" Mrs Thomas stood in the doorway, somehow lacking authority in her dressing-gown, her face pale and colourless without the usual make-up.

Silently the two boys climbed into their beds and the teacher retreated, closing the door behind her.

"Did you see her pyjamas?" Jonathan said, and they both giggled.

Soon it was evident by Andrew's regular breathing that he was asleep. Despite his tiredness Jonathan lay awake for some time staring into the dark and clutching the duvet round his chin, although the room wasn't cold.

How different from home, he thought. It was so quiet in the mountains, not like his room over the main road with traffic passing all night and a street lamp shining directly in, despite the thick curtains his mum had put up.

What would she be doing now, all alone? She'd insisted he still came on the ski-ing trip even though she couldn't afford it now. Should he have absolutely refused to come? But he'd so much wanted to be a part of the school trip, and to go ski-ing again.

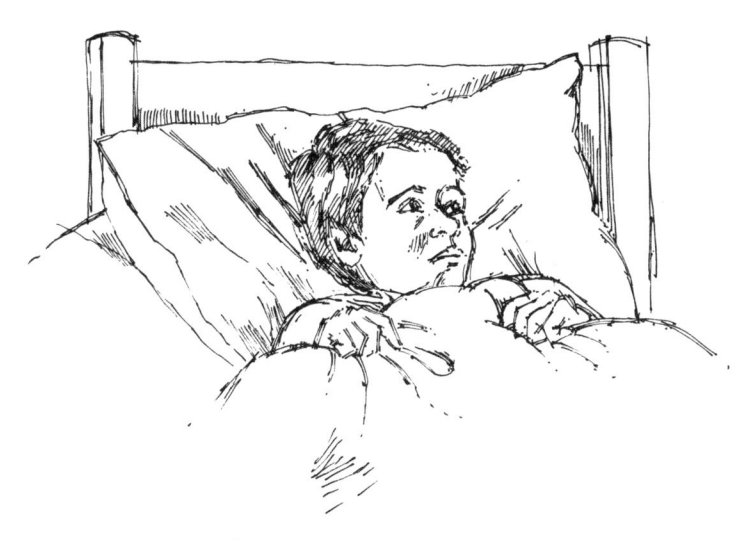

As Jonathan thought of home he began to half wish he was there. A wave of home-sickness swept over him and he turned onto his side trying to shake it off.

If he was at home he wouldn't have to face doing a black run with Melanie Jackson watching and laughing at him.

He pictured the colour definitions in the ski brochure.

Blue – easy, red – medium, black – difficult.

He wished there were no black runs here.

But there were.

It was a dog whining that woke him. That's silly, he thought, sleepily. No dog would be out there roaming about. He forced one eye open and looked at the luminous figures on his watch. Two-thirty.

There it was again. A faint, pityful whining.

"Andrew!" he whispered, wide awake now. There was no sound or movement from the other bed. Jonathan flung back the duvet and tiptoed over to the window. The night was dark. No stars, nothing to be seen. All was quiet now.

He slid back the balcony door a little way and shivered as the cold air hit him.

Then he heard a voice distant but clear in the still air.

"Barr – ee."

The sound echoed eerily through the valley and then there was silence again. Jonathan waited another minute and when he was unable to bear the cold any more he closed the door and clambered back into bed.

Who or what was out there on the mountain at this time of night?

Chapter 2

ANDREW WAS already climbing into his ski suit when Jonathan awoke the next morning.

"Hey, why didn't you wake me?"

Andrew shrugged. "Plenty of time. Breakfast isn't until eight o'clock." And he busied himself getting gloves and goggles together.

Jonathan washed and dressed hurriedly. He, too, was really looking forward to getting on the slopes. Things always seemed better in daylight.

"Did you hear that dog whining last night?" he said, brushing his fine fair hair vigorously until it crackled and stood on end.

"A dog? Out there at night? Don't be daft." Andrew didn't sound very interested.

"I'm sure it was a dog. I got up and opened the balcony door and then someone called out 'Barry'."

"You were dreaming. Come on, let's go."

After breakfast the teachers took the children down to the ski and boot room. As usual, the voice of Melanie Jackson could be heard above the rest.

"I've got my own boots. I only need skis." And she lifted a boot onto the counter to be fitted for the skis.

For some time the room was filled

with excited voices, the clumping of heavy ski boots and snap of clips. The fixings on the skis were adjusted to fit the boots by the two men behind the counter, and the safety releases were tested to make sure the boots would come out of the skis in a fall or sudden jolt and the wearer would not break or twist a leg. Ski poles were measured for correct height and handed out.

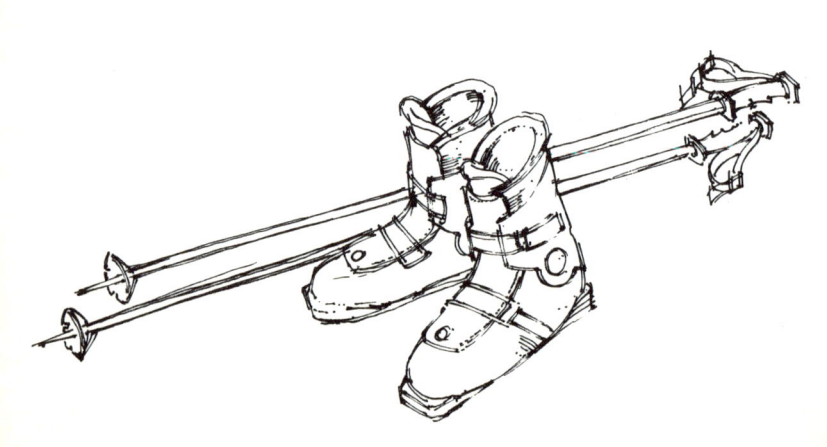

Then Mr Fredericks banged his fist on the counter.

"Quiet!" he roared. The noise gradually subsided.

"Right," he said. "As soon as you're kitted out, make your way down to the ski school next to the chairlift station. Those who can ski down do so, and those who can't will have to walk down the road carrying their skis. Keep in your groups. Don't go off alone, and be careful. And, have fun!"

With that, he picked up his own skis and went out of the door followed by a boot-stomping, ski-clacking crowd.

Jonathan was last and Mrs Thomas waited patiently for him. He'd had trouble finding a comfortable pair of boots and now the man was adjusting his skis. He looked round to see if

Andrew had waited but there was no sign of him.

"You are ready to go now," said the man, handing Jonathan his skis and sticks. It didn't take him long to snap his feet into his skis and he was off down the short slope. The wind on his face was exhilarating and he felt very happy.

Mr Fredericks was sorting the children into different groups for ski lessons when Jonathan arrived. The absolute beginners were already divided into two groups and heading off to a gentle slope nearby with their ski teachers. Jonathan was sent with the remainder, those who had skied before, to the chairlift.

He joined the queue shuffling towards the double chairs. That meant two people rode together side by side. He looked round. George Maitland was next to him, his nose and lips white with cream.

Jonathan giggled. "You look like a clown."

George's freckled face broke into a grin. "Better safe than sorry," he said. "I burn if I just look at the sun. By the way, if you're looking for Andrew he said he'd see you up top."

"Hm. Fine friend he is. Want to share the chairlift?"

George nodded but as the queue narrowed down the two boys became separated and Jonathan found himself next to Melanie.

She smiled in a friendly way. "Isn't it great?" she enthused about nothing in particular.

Their turn came and they moved forward to stand in position, skis straight ahead, watching over their shoulders as the chairs came round the big cable wheel and towards them. They sat down and were whisked away. Jonathan reached up to pull down the safety bar.

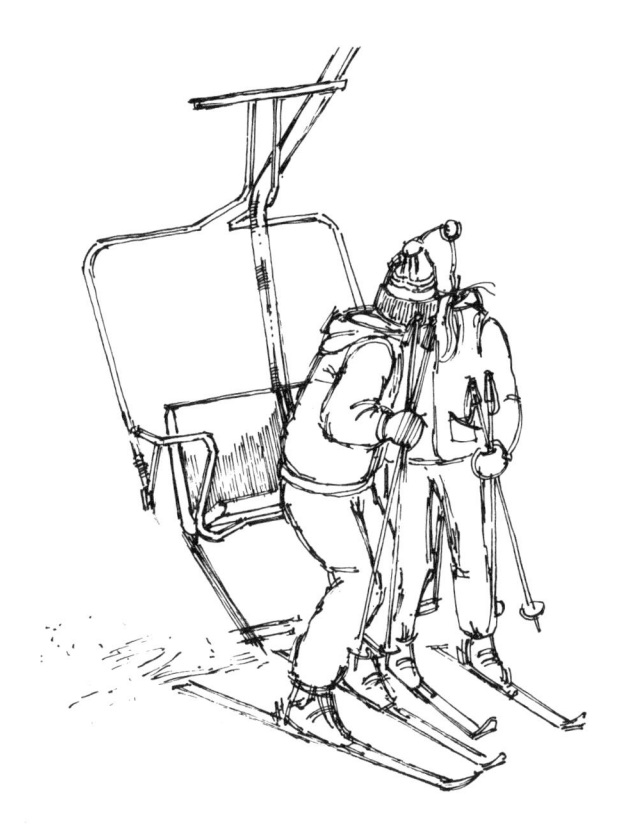

Neither of them spoke for some time as they glided over the slopes and it was only after they'd rattled over the first pylon that Melanie said:

"I wish I lived in Switzerland, don't you? Then I'd be able to ski all winter."

"Yeah."

But it wouldn't just be because of the ski-ing, Jonathan thought. The mountains fascinated him. They were beautiful yet powerful, threatening. They frightened him a little. It was so peaceful and there was a sort of freedom he'd never felt before.

They rattled over another pylon and Melanie slipped her skis off the footrest and began to swing them backwards and forwards causing the chairs to swing as well.

Jonathan gripped the bar tighter as if to try to steady it.

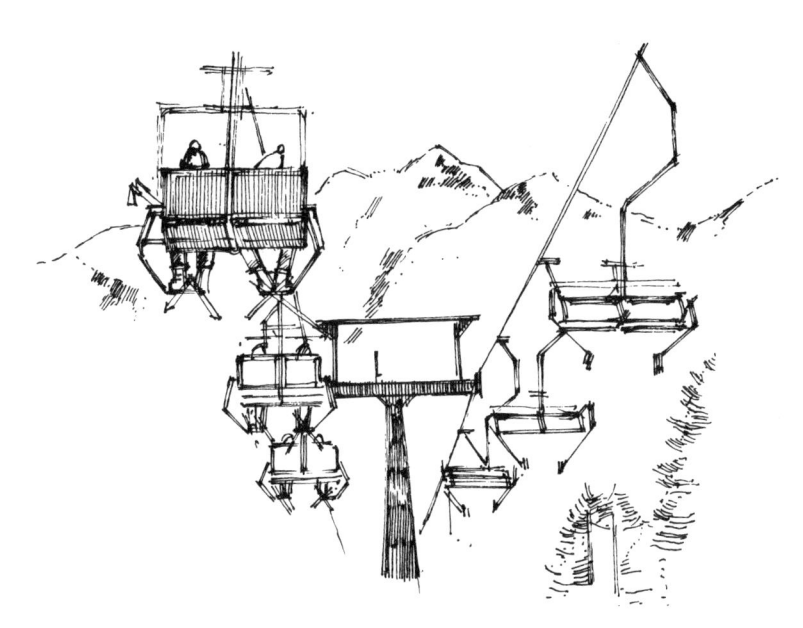

"Didn't you see what that sign said on the pylon?"

"No, what?"

"*Défence de balancer.*"

Melanie wrinkled up her nose, not comprehending.

"No swinging. The cable might jump off the little wheels."

She gave a disgusted snort but nevertheless put her feet back on the bar.

"Thank goodness we won't be in the same class," she said, nastily. "I can't stand people who won't take any risks. They slow the class down and I don't like waiting for anybody."

Jonathan was glad too but didn't answer. They were arriving at the top of the lift now and he raised the safety bar. Then as their skis touched the ground, they skied off.

Andrew was there, leaning on one pole and grinning as he saw who Jonathan had shared the lift with.

"You could have waited for me," moaned Jonathan, crossly. "I had to come up with that awful Melanie."

"Sorry." Andrew dug his poles in the snow. "Our class is over here."

Jonathan soon forgot his crossness as they joined the class and it was only later that his enjoyment was again spoilt by the interfering Melanie.

He was going up on a drag lift, the metal pole with the plastic disc on the end comfortably between his legs, hauling him up the slope. He felt confident on the lifts this year. As long as you kept your skis straight in the tracks and didn't let them wander, it was quite easy really.

As he watched the points of his skis gliding effortlessly up the slope there was a sudden swish and someone flashed across the tracks immediately in front of him. One of his skis turned inwards and he was over, the lift pole continuing its journey without him.

Jonathan quickly rolled off the tracks and out of the way of the person coming behind and then he stared at the retreating figure in an orange anorak. He knew quite well who it was. Trust her to wear a conspicuous colour like that.

"I'll get you!" he shouted after her, picking himself up and ski-ing down to the starting point again.

After dinner that evening there'd been a disco and everyone was absolutely exhausted by the time they went to bed. Even Jonathan had dropped straight off to sleep without a single thought of home.

He awoke some time later to someone shaking his shoulder. Andrew's dark shape loomed over him.

"I heard it," he whispered. "The dog whining."

It came again then, but louder than the previous night. A pityful whining followed by a long howl which wrenched at the hearts of both boys in its utter misery.

They slipped on anoraks and shoes and quietly sliding open the balcony door, stepped out into the cold night.

There was a full moon. They leaned out over the balcony and peered across the slope.

There, about twenty metres from them stood a huge dog, its eyes glinting as they caught the light from the moon. He was looking straight at them.

"It's a St Bernard," whispered Jonathan. "They used to use them for rescuing people from avalanches."

He felt rather than saw Andrew nod. The dog walked towards them a little, its eyes still fixed on them. It was then that they noticed a darker ragged patch on the brown fur of his head. From the patch something dripped slowly but regularly onto the snow.

"I think he's hurt," gasped Andrew,

"he's bleeding." He grasped Jonathan's arm tightly. "Come on, let's go and get him."

They opened the bedroom door and crept out into the corridor. No one else seemed to have heard anything and the hotel was silent.

The two boys went downstairs, through the lounge to the big front door and unbolted it as quietly as they could. They slipped out and round the hotel, across the small car park, the snow squeaking loudly under foot.

When they reached the slope under their balcony the moon had gone behind a cloud, and it was difficult to see anything except the outline of the mountains against the sky, and the darker shapes of trees further across the mountainside.

After a long, cold five minutes the moon came out again. But there was no sign of the dog. They walked over to the approximate spot where he'd been standing and looked carefully round in every direction.

"Gone," sighed Jonathan, "poor thing. Why didn't he wait? We could have helped him. He was bleeding pretty badly, Andrew."

"I know. A head wound too. We'd better tell Mr Fredericks in the morning."

They turned and trudged back towards the hotel door, shivering now in only pyjamas and anoraks. As they reached the entrance a voice echoed through the trees making them jump and clutch at each other.

"*Barr – ee.*"

It was a hollow, haunting sound which remained ringing in their ears and prevented sleep coming for quite some time.

Chapter 3

MR FREDERICKS listened intently to the boys' story the next morning as they stood in reception, waiting for the dining room to open for breakfast.

The hotel manager was leaning on his elbows on the desk and shaking his head. "I can't understand it. No one in this village has a St Bernard. The nearest ones that I know of are at the Hospice at the top of the St Bernard Pass, and that's too far away for the dogs to roam. Besides, they are only let out for exercise by the monks – and certainly not at night time."

"You say he was wounded?" put in the headmaster.

The boys nodded. "We could see the blood dripping onto the snow."

"It hasn't snowed during the night. Let's go and see."

They all went out of the hotel and followed the boys' footprints of the night before which were clearly visible and frozen like moulds.

The footprints led out into the middle of the slope and then ended in a churned-up patch of snow where they'd stopped to look around for the dog.

There was no sign of any blood or any other marks in the snow at all. It stretched right to the trees, smooth and undisturbed.

Andrew frowned. "We really did see him, Sir. It was moonlight. We saw him clearly – and heard him."

Mr Fredericks said nothing and Jonathan knew he didn't believe them. But the manager smiled understandingly.

"Nevertheless," he said, "I will telephone the Hospice to try to clear up the mystery."

Back in reception he ran his finger down a list of numbers pinned to the wall, and reached for the phone.

"Allo?" He continued the conversation in rapid French which the boys couldn't follow. Then he held out the phone. "You tell your story. Brother Jean speaks English very well."

Jonathan took the phone. "Jonathan Cave speaking."

"Hello Jonathan. Monsieur Denaux tells me you and your friend saw a St Bernard near the hotel last night?" Brother Jean's voice was kind.

"Yes. He was whining just under our balcony."

"Are you sure it was a St Bernard?"

"Oh yes. It was very big, brown and white. I've seen lots of pictures of them and we saw a stuffed one at the Natural History Museum last month."

"Well now," said the monk, "we do have about ten dogs here but they are always kept in their house at night and we take them for walks during the day. Of course they are not used for rescuing people any more. Now that we have the tunnel the Pass is closed for eight months of the year. We really only keep them for the tourists in the summer time."

"Do you have one called Barry?" asked Jonathan.

The monk hesitated slightly before answering. "Yes. Why?"

"Because we heard someone calling his name."

There was no reply so Jonathan continued. "And he was hurt. Badly hurt on the head, and bleeding."

The pause was longer this time. So long in fact that Jonathan thought they'd been cut off.

"Hello?" he said.

Brother Jean's voice sounded different when he spoke again. A little anxious Jonathan thought, or nervous.

"All our dogs are quite safe," he said, "but be careful my son, be very careful."

The line clicked and he was gone. Jonathan slowly put down the receiver and gave Andrew a look which said "I'll tell you later".

"He says all their dogs are there and none are wounded." He looked at the manager. "Thank you for phoning."

The manager nodded his head slightly and the two boys and their headmaster went in silence to the breakfast table.

"What did he say?" Andrew asked eagerly as they went up in the chairlift later on.

"It was a bit funny," said Jonathan slowly. "He was very chatty and

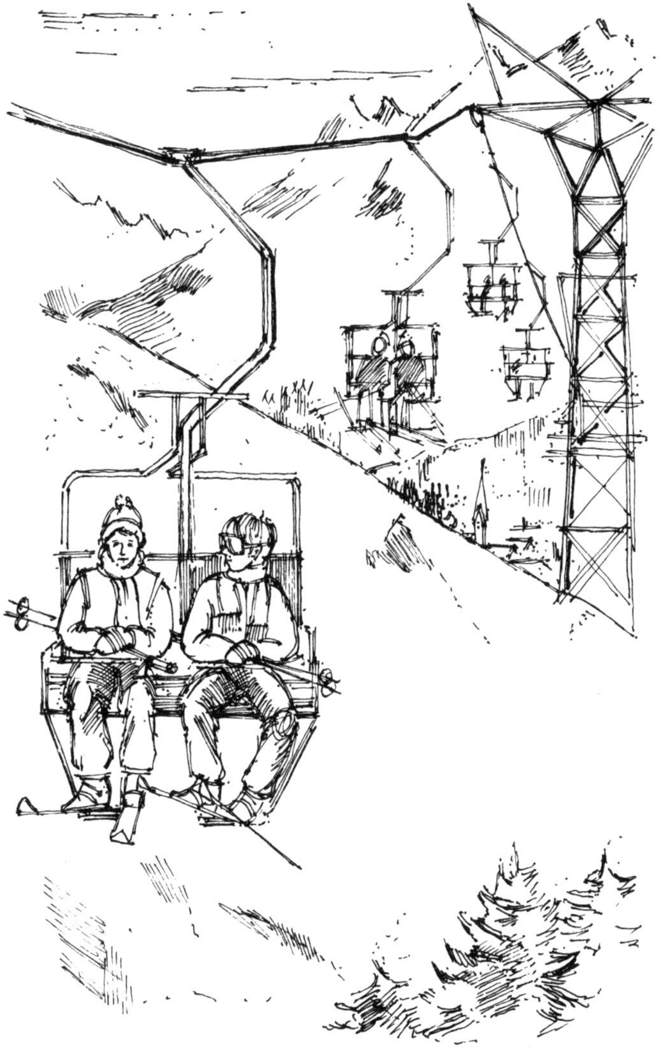

friendly at first but when I mentioned the name 'Barry' and that he was wounded he didn't answer. I could hear him breathing but he didn't speak for a long time and then he sounded sort of worried and said 'be careful' twice and hung up."

"How odd. Perhaps he didn't understand you very well."

"Oh he did. He spoke perfect English." Jonathan looked at his friend.

"We really did see the dog, didn't we?"

Andrew nodded vigorously. "Yes we did," he said emphatically.

They joined their class and stood in line, trying to concentrate on their ski teacher, Alain, as he demonstrated parallel turns.

Jonathan found his mind constantly

wandering. They *had* seen a wounded dog, there was no question about it. But where was he now? Perhaps already dead. And how was it that no one else had heard him?

He poked at the snow with his stick. It was annoying when you knew something was true but no one believed you.

Dad would have believed him. He wouldn't have dismissed it just because there was no proof. Dad liked mysteries. He must tell him about it when he got home.

No he wouldn't.

In all the excitement he hadn't thought about home. Dad wasn't there any more. Wasn't there. Jonathan's mouth went dry and he felt sick. He could tell Dad when he next visited him. Of course he could. He still had a mum and a dad but – they didn't live together any more.

Suddenly he was aware that he was at the top of the line and it was his turn to ski down, imitating the teacher's turns, in front of the class.

He set off.

"Lean more out!" yelled Alain.

"Bend your knees. Good."

Andrew was next.

"Good!" shouted Alain. "Very good!"

Andrew swished to a stop beside Jonathan, grinning broadly at the praise.

"You're doing okay, Andrew."

"Thanks," he said. "It's easy when you get the hang of it."

That afternoon when ski school was over the class began to disperse. Mrs Thomas was organising a small trip to the village. Shall we do one more run before the lifts close?" whispered Andrew.

Jonathan hesitated.

"We're not supposed to go up on our own, and I did want to go to the village to get Mum a present. What time do the shops close?"

"Dunno," Andrew shrugged, "but you can do that another day. And we'll be down in half an hour. Nobody will know we've been. Nobody'll miss us."

"All right. Let's do the number four. It's a nice easy one."

Ten minutes later they skied off the drag lift and looked at the signpost in front of them. Someone else was standing there looking at it too. She turned and frowned at them.

"Look at that!" said Melanie Jackson, "they've closed the number three. Seeing as you're so good at French, what does that sign say?" She glared crossly at Jonathan as if it was his fault.

"*Fermé. Danger d'avalanches*," he read. "It's closed because there's a risk of avalanches."

"I like that run," she said petulantly.

"It was all right this morning. I'm going down." And she skied to the wooden barrier and bent to go underneath it.

"Melanie, you can't! Come back!" cried Andrew. "Come and do the number four with us, it's getting late!"

"I'm going down here. You go down

your easy blue run," she scoffed, and set off down the slope.

Andrew looked at Jonathan.

"She's mad! There's nobody on that run and even the *piste* service won't be going down." He referred to the men who went down the slopes at the end of the day to make sure that no one was hurt or stranded.

Jonathan looked at his friend's worried face. He knew what Andrew was going to say next.

"We'd better go after her. Come on. It's only a red run, not too difficult. It'll be okay."

Jonathan felt the old panic feeling grow inside him again and he started to refuse, but Andrew was already ducking under the barrier so he knew that he had to go too.

They set off down the silent slope. The sun had disappeared behind a cloud and a wind blew suddenly ice-cold into their faces.

Chapter 4

IT FELT strange and eerie ski-ing alone down a slope. Usually the *pistes* were alive with the swish and scrape of skis, the laughter and squeals of excitement. They were colourful and busy.

But here, with a steep slope towering to their left and the woods on their right, the silence was total except for the whispering of their own skis as they zig-zagged down the wide ledge.

They could have been a hundred

miles from civilisation here, with the trees blocking their view of the valley and village. It was the sort of isolation and peacefulness that Jonathan would normally have enjoyed, but not now. Not with the constant threat of an avalanche occurring and the knowledge that they weren't supposed to be on this run at all, or any run for that matter. After ski school they were only allowed to go on the nursery slopes, Mr Fredericks had said, unless they had an adult with them.

"There she is!" Andrew's voice penetrated his thoughts and to Jonathan's horror he cupped his hands and yelled.

"Me – lan – ie!"

"Don't shout!" Jonathan hissed, sliding to a stop. "A noise can start an avalanche!"

Andrew snapped his mouth shut and stared back at his friend with fear in his eyes. Jonathan looked beyond and saw that Melanie had stopped as well. He was too far away to see her face but knew by the whole attitude of her body that she was furious, probably by the fact that they had followed her.

Andrew was still motionless and silent as if afraid that another move on his part would certainly be disastrous.

"Come on," Jonathan said quietly, "we might as well catch up with her."

They set off again, annoyed to see that Melanie hadn't waited for them.

"I think she's cross that we followed," panted Jonathan. "She wanted to have something to show off about."

Andrew just nodded and they continued in silence for several minutes. There she was again, a splash of orange approaching the next corner.

It was then that they were aware of a noise. Just a low distant rumble.

They stopped and Andrew slowly lifted his head to look up the mountain. He squinted and then his eyes widened and, as Jonathan watched, a look of sheer terror slowly spread across his face.

"Oh no!" he whispered, "Oh no!"

Jonathan forced himself to follow his friend's gaze upwards. A small plume of white had risen above the highest ridge. He remembered a talk they'd had before the trip and knew that it meant one thing.

An avalanche had begun.

Frantically they looked around for some shelter or means of escape but the only way they could go was on down the ledge and hope to get out of the avalanche's path. They were dimly aware that Melanie had seen it too and was racing onward.

Jabbing their poles viciously into the snow they pushed off, straight down now, no zig-zagging, faster and faster, praying that they didn't fall.

The rumble became a roar. And then they saw it. A great mass of snow sliding and bouncing and rolling towards them. Panic-stricken they both had the same idea and slid off the ledge into the trees. Then each encircled a tree with his arms, closed his eyes, and waited to be engulfed by the great white tidal wave.

The roar gradually lessened, and at last stopped. The boys opened their eyes and stared disbelievingly. Just above their part of the ledge the slope levelled out quite a lot and the avalanche had spent most of its energy there. Some had spilt over onto the ledge but there was still room to ski.

Silently, they side-stepped back up onto the *piste* and slowly skied forward, shaken and shocked by their narrow escape.

"Melanie," Jonathan breathed.

They rounded the next corner where they'd last seen her, and stopped. This section hadn't been so lucky. The slope above was steeper therefore the snow had not been slowed down but had hurtled over onto the ledge. A chaotic jumble of snow blocked their way.

Melanie Jackson was nowhere to be seen.

Chapter 5

FOR A few seconds the boys looked at the heap of snow in front of them, the same thought in both their minds. Somewhere underneath was Melanie, but where, and how could they get her out in time?

To make matters worse, a thick cloud had come down and it was beginning to snow so that everything looked blank white, except for the trees on their right and the great chunks of avalanche snow showing through in parts as darker shades of grey.

They stepped forward gingerly onto the loose chunky snow. It was difficult to balance as smaller lumps and powder gave way under their skis.

"This is no good," said Jonathan. "We're not getting anywhere. Do you think it would be better to skirt round through the trees? Perhaps she was pushed forward by the snow and isn't buried." He tried to sound hopeful. If she was buried, how long could she survive? . . . if she was alive at all . . . He pushed that thought firmly to the back of his mind.

"Do you think I . . . my shout . . . " began Andrew, his shoulders slumped forward dejectedly.

Jonathan shook his head as he pulled on his anorak hood.

"Of course not. It was ages after. But come on, we have to try to find her. If she's buried under that lot she'll suffocate."

Andrew seemed to brighten up a little as the burden of guilt was lifted from him. They made their way back into the trees again, side-stepping down the steep slope and grasping at trees for support. The snow was deep here, and the going was slow.

"Do you think it's safe to shout?" asked Andrew.

"Not too loudly."

They began calling as they went.

"Me – lan – ie!"

Their voices echoed through the trees. But there was no answering call. Their eyes constantly searched the whiteness around them.

"We're nearly at the other side." Andrew didn't voice the thought that was in both their minds. What if they got to the other side and still hadn't found her? How do you begin to look for someone buried under the snow?

It was Jonathan who saw the splash of orange at the edge of the ledge and in the split second before he alerted Andrew he reflected on the fact that if she hadn't been wearing a bright colour they may never have found her.

She was lying on her back across the slope, the ski sticks still attached to her wrists by their straps. A huge chunk of snow was resting on her right leg which seemed to be bent at a funny angle. There was no sign of her skis.

"She's alive but she's unconscious,"

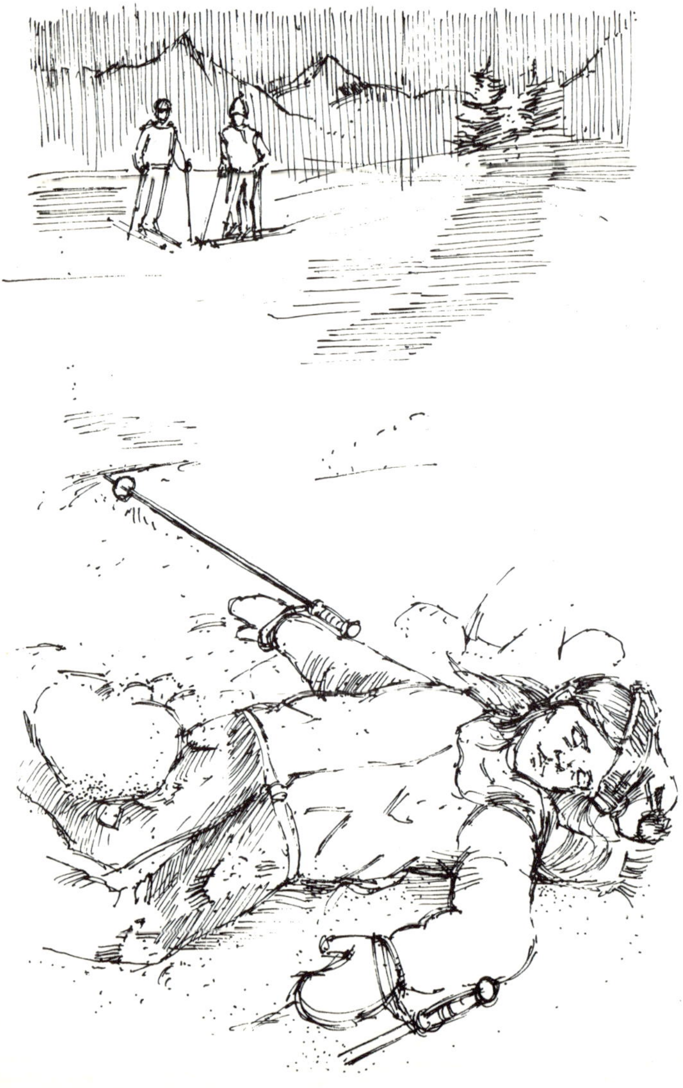

said Jonathan, "I can just see her breathing."

Andrew just nodded.

Jonathan glanced at his friend. "Look at her leg. Do you think it's broken?"

Andrew nodded again as Jonathan bent to release his skis.

"We'd better try to get this chunk of snow off her leg."

The piece of frozen snow was very heavy but the boys knew that they had to remove it before she came round. The pain of the broken leg would be bad enough without a weight like that on it.

At last it rolled off and the boys stood up slowly, sweating despite the cold dampness around them.

"I don't know anything about what

to do with broken legs." Jonathan stared down at it. "We'd better just leave it and one of us stay with her while the other goes for help. You're a better skier than me, Andrew."

"N . . . no, not me, Jon. Please . . . I can't."

Jonathan looked at his friend's face in amazement. It was white and crumpled with fear. He'd never seen him like this before. Andrew was the one who always jumped into everything with both feet without thinking first, but now, when courage and daring were needed, he didn't want to go. That's why he'd been so quiet for the last few minutes.

"Okay then," Jonathan said quietly, removing his anorak. "Look, we'd better cover her with our anoraks. I'll be as quick as I can."

He knocked the snow off the bottom of his boots and one by one clicked them into his skis, feeling far less confident than he sounded. He knew, deep down, that he felt just the same as his friend, but one of them had to go, otherwise Melanie would die in the cold.

"See yer," he said softly, and set off.

Jonathan was aware that speed was essential but it was difficult to see where he was going in the foggy whiteness. It was snowing quite heavily now, big flakes drifting straight down. The wind had dropped fortunately. He pushed on, staring at the ground in front of the two points of his skis.

Where he left the ski track he didn't know but he was suddenly aware that he was in deep snow and the slope was steeper. He stopped in a panic and then looked around. Perhaps the ski *piste* had turned to the left and he'd just gone straight on. If he side-stepped up to the left then, he should meet it again.

After five minutes of tiring climbing he knew he was lost. He had no idea which way the village was. If he kept going he could end up in some remote valley – or worse, over a precipice.

Jonathan leaned over his sticks in despair and warm tears dripped onto the snow. The only thing he could do was wait until the fog lifted – and that might not be until morning.

A slight noise broke the silence and he looked up, blinking his tears away. There, about five metres in front of him, stood the St Bernard.

"Barry!" Jonathan whispered.

The dog's tail moved slightly and he gave another small whine, then started walking ahead, looking back every few steps. The wound looked just as bad but didn't seem to bother him.

Jonathan brushed his gloved hand across his eyes and slid forward after him. The dog never came any closer but constantly made sure that he was following. They were going more across the slope than down and even that was difficult for Jonathan, who wasn't used to deep-snow ski-ing. Once his skis got going too fast and he couldn't straighten them so he sat down in the snow to stop.

Finally, he noticed the fog thinning out and the snow underfoot becoming firmer.

At last he could see the village down below.

As he came out into the clear he heard a voice calling.

"*Bar – ree.*"

He looked quickly to the left and high on a ridge stood a grey figure, his robes gently moving in the breeze.

When Jonathan looked back, the dog had gone. There below him was the village, deep in shadow now. He took a deep breath of relief but it caught in his throat as he looked at the slope between him and safety.

It was most definitely a black run.

Chapter 6

JONATHAN SAT down in the snow staring through his tears at the slope in front of him.

He couldn't do it. He'd fall, and slide down and down . . .

It was much steeper than he'd ever done before and the bumps formed between the ski tracks were enormous and hard and slippery. The tracks between the bumps were steep and narrow.

Good skiers would think nothing of it. He'd seen them bouncing lightly and effortlessly this way and that, never gaining speed, always in control. But he was only a beginner really.

He couldn't do it.

Why had they disobeyed the rules and gone for another run? Why had that stupid Melanie Jackson gone onto that closed slope? Well, he knew why. Because she was a show-off. He hated her. She didn't deserve rescuing. "I don't like waiting for anybody," she'd said. Well, now she was waiting wasn't she? For him, Jonathan, to fetch help. Her life depended on him.

The thought jolted Jonathan to his senses. He did have a responsibility to her and to Andrew. Somehow – for his own sake too – he had to get down to the village for help.

If he just sat here all night they might all die.

Jonathan struggled to his feet slowly, pushing himself up with his sticks and again wiping his tears with his gloved hand. He'd never felt so alone in all his life. Even the dog had gone. But he'd done his job, guided him out of the fog and onto a *piste*. From now on no one could help him except himself.

He took a deep breath and slid forward, eyes scanning the slope for a good bump to turn on. There. That one. Stem out with the uphill ski, transfer weight to it. He was round!

Now his skis were running fast down the steep track. He braked and braked.

Slower now. Don't look down. Don't look at how steep it is. Don't think about having to cross the fall line with every turn. Up, relieve the weight, weight on the lower ski. Another turn done.

He stopped for a moment to get his breath. A mistake. It took courage to go again. But he must go on. The ski teacher's words echoed in his head. Keep knees bent, lean out, weight on downhill ski. Jonathan tried to concentrate his whole attention on "listening" to Alain's voice. It wasn't difficult to imagine it. Everyone made the same mistakes. Those teachers must get fed up with saying the same things over and over . . .

Now he was going too fast! Brake! Brake! Too late. He ran straight into a bump and he was over, sliding down head first. He dragged his sticks desperately in the snow to try to slow himself down. It seemed as if he was never going to stop.

Then at last, he did. He lay sprawled in the snow for a few seconds and then swung his feet round so that they were across the slope. His legs felt like jelly as he hauled himself up. One ski had come off. He looked around. If he couldn't find it he'd have to walk down – and that would be worse.

There it was, its little brakes sticking into the snow. He hobbled over, picked it up and laid it beside his foot. The sole of the boot was caked with snow so, leaning on one stick and standing on one ski, he lifted his right foot and chipped away at the snow with the other stick until it was clear enough to click into the ski.

That done, Jonathan looked around him again. He had slid down about five metres. Not too far to go now but his legs felt weak and would hardly support him or do what he wanted them to.

How he wished and wished he was safe at home.

Another turn done. Then he fell again but didn't lose a ski.

At last the slope levelled out a little, and soon joined the blue run which passed the hotel on its way to the chairlift and ski school. Jonathan sped down the last bit right up to the front door of the hotel. He snapped his feet out of his skis and ran as best he could in ski boots, through the lounge to the reception desk, leaving clods of dirty snow all over the carpet.

Mr Fredericks was talking to the manager. They both looked worried.

"Help!" gasped Jonathan, almost collapsing at their feet with sheer exhaustion. "Melanie! Andrew!"

"What! Where are they? What's happened?" urged Mr Fredericks, grasping Jonathan and sitting him down. "The *piste* service is out looking for you! We've been worried sick—"

"An avalanche," he gasped. On the number three. Melanie's hurt." He sank back into the chair gratefully.

"But what were you doing . . . never mind." The headmaster turned to the manager who was already on the phone, alerting the hospital.

Children were crowding around Jonathan.

"Someone go to the ski room and fetch his ordinary boots," ordered Mr Fredericks, and started unclipping Jonathan's ski boots. "Let's get you into some warm, dry clothes. You might be best to go to bed."

Jonathan opened his eyes weakly. Bed? He had to make sure that Andrew and Melanie were safe first.

A waitress thrust a steaming glass of red liquid into his hands.

"*Vin chaud*," she said, "to warm you."

Jonathan sipped the hot spiced wine and felt the warmth revive him a little.

"Please let me go with the emergency service, Sir."

Mr Fredericks stared thoughtfully at him for a few moments.

"All right, Jon," he said, slipping the warm, soft boots onto the boy's feet. "Could you tell how badly Melanie was hurt?"

"Well, she was unconscious and I think she's broken her leg."

The headmaster nodded, his normally cheerful face drawn and anxious.

Soon the rescue team were on the snowcat churning straight up the slope, red light flashing. Normally Jonathan would have been delighted at having a ride on one of these incredible vehicles but now he was too tired to care and just wanted to find his friends.

It had stopped snowing as they reached the ledge and the cloud had lifted a little.

"Just round the next bend I think." Jonathan peered out through the cab window. "There!" He pointed up the slope to where the main part of the avalanche could be seen.

Andrew had heard them coming and was standing up waving his arms about as they rounded the bend. The driver stopped the cat a few metres away and he and another man jumped down with a stretcher and carried it to where Melanie was lying. Jonathan saw that she was conscious now and smiling weakly as the men approached but she cried out in pain as they lifted her onto the stretcher and strapped her in.

Jonathan rode back in the cab with her, holding the stretcher, while the second man and Andrew, who had also been wrapped in a large blanket, sat in the back.

"Thank you," whispered Melanie, smiling up at Jonathan. "And I'm sorry."

"It's okay."

"How did you find your way down – in the fog?"

"The dog," he said. And then realising that she knew nothing about it, he told her how the howling had woken them and they had seen it out in the snow.

Melanie screwed up her face with pain as the snowcat jolted over a bump.

"I heard it too," she muttered, "but I thought it was a wolf . . . " Her voice trailed off and her eyes closed for a minute or two. Then they opened again.

"Did he lead you right down to the hotel?"

"No, just out of the fog and onto the *piste* – the number six."

A small smile crept over Melanie's face but it was a friendly smile.

"So," she whispered, "you've done a black run?"

"Yes," he said, proudly. "I have." And for some reason he suddenly felt very happy and confident in himself.

Of course the whole story had to be told again, not once but several times. Everyone sat spellbound as he described the oncoming avalanche, but it was the dog which interested them most.

Mr Fredericks had said nothing more about their ski-ing alone or being on a closed run, they'd learnt their lesson the hard way, but now he spoke.

"That dog again," he said, "we've got to get to the bottom of this." But the manager was already on the phone to the Hospice once more. He spoke to someone there for a moment and then, as he listened to the reply, a strange look came over his face and he silently handed the receiver over to Jonathan. The whole room was silent, looking on, almost holding its breath as Jonathan listened to the monk's story.

"During the last century," said Brother Jean, "we had many St Bernards here. People constantly became lost or stranded and needed rescuing.

"In 1800 a remarkable dog was born.

He was called Barry from the word *bari* meaning 'little bear'. He was an expert at finding people buried under the snow and during the twelve years he worked here he rescued forty people.

"Unfortunately the forty-first person he was about to rescue thought he really was a bear and hit him on the head with an ice-axe. Poor Barry was fatally wounded and died soon after, but ever since then we have given the best dog born each year the name 'Barry', in memory of this wonderful dog."

"But . . ." began Jonathan, bewildered.

"A few years ago," continued the monk, "someone else reported seeing a wounded dog – just like you did – and also hearing the name Barry called.

Two days later that person was killed in an avalanche."

"We thought it was coincidence but now we are sure. Barry came to warn you. It was always believed that they could predict avalanches. The dog you saw then, Jonathan, was the spirit of the great Barry."

Jonathan could hardly speak but he thanked the monk and put down the receiver. Then he turned slowly, stunned, to his waiting audience.

"It was a ghost," he said, "a ghost dog saved our lives."

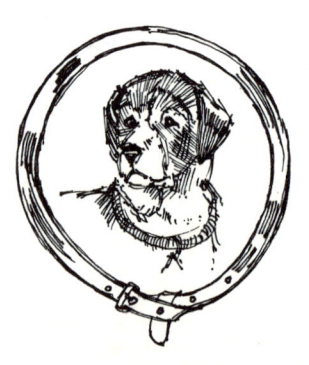